THE JACK OF ONE TRADE

OTHER BOOKS BY RYAN EIDSON

Fiction
A Couple With Common Cents

Nonfiction
Money Management For Cross-Cultural Workers

THE JACK OF ONE TRADE
A Story About Career Change

RYAN EIDSON

COPPER COIN PRESS

THE JACK OF ONE TRADE
A Story About Career Change

© 2018 Ryan Eidson

Published in Moberly, Missouri by Copper Coin Press.

ISBN 978-0-98852-943-4 paperback

Editing and layout by
Susan White, The Scribe's Closet Publications
www.thescribesclosetpublications.com

Cover design by
Rachel Lopez
www.r2cdesign.com

Interior hammer image modified from: "Hammer Marteau" by flickr user eurok. Creative Commons 2.0 Attribution License.

To Abigail

May you discover your strengths
and use them to serve others.

CONTENTS

"Whatever your hands find to do,
do with all your strength."
—**Ecclesiastes** 9:10 (HCSB)

"You can't be 'anything you want,' but you can be
something even better: the best version of you."
—**Jon Acuff,** *Start*, p. 115

"What drives progress is increased specialization
and increased trade."
—**Richard Koch,** *The Natural Laws of Business,* p. 98

INTRODUCTION

Are you ready to change careers? Are you thinking about starting your own business, leaping into self-employment?

Are you struggling to discover what you're really good at doing?

Or are you talented in several ways and unsure of which direction to go?

Wherever you are in your journey of work, this story will inspire you to consider what it is that you do best, and to seek a great mentor to help you in your journey.

Thank you for reading. If you find this book helpful, please share it with others.

Turbulence

Jack, wake up! We're almost ready to land!"

Tabitha shook her husband. A flight attendant walked down the aisle to make sure everyone was prepared for the landing.

"Sir? Excuse me, sir, we are preparing to land," she said. "Please put your seat in its upright position, and fasten your seat belt."

Jack came to at the sound of the unfamiliar voice. "Sorry, ma'am." He gave his wife an eyes-half-open look as he slowly adjusted his seat.

Immediately, he was jolted wide awake. They grabbed the arms of their seats as their stomachs hit their throats. They heard the luggage in the compartments above them bounce around.

The captain announced over the intercom, "Sorry about that, folks. We have encountered unexpected turbulence. A thunderstorm is brewing, but we'll have you on the ground in about 15 minutes."

"Ugh, I don't feel so good!" Katie moaned.

Kyle reached for the bag in the seat pocket, tore off the top and opened it, then handed it to his sister. "If it's coming, make sure you get it in that bag! I don't want you sick all over me!"

"Katie," her mother admonished, "that's why I told you to not be snacking the whole time we're on the plane. I know you are excited at your first flight, but we still have another longer one ahead."

The plane shook a few more minutes before they touched down at Houston.

"I am so glad to be on the ground," Katie breathed deeply. "I almost spewed everywhere."

"That would've been some way to start our family vacation," Kyle rolled his eyes. "Now, give me some space to play my game." He was always doing something on his phone, yet only used it *as* a phone when his parents called him.

As the Cundiff family walked into the terminal, Tabitha checked the status of their connecting flight to Mexico City. "We're still right on time," she announced. "We have about one hour until we board our next flight. Everyone have their stuff ready?"

"Sure looks like we do!" Jack smacked her hand in a high five. "Thanks for staying so organized, honey."

"Just doing what I do best, Jack. Quick, we want to make sure we catch our connection."

As the four of them ran toward the international terminal, the status board for flight 273 to Mexico City changed from *on time* to *delayed*.

Delayed

W hat do you mean we're delayed?" Kyle exclaimed. "The screen said 'On Time' just a few minutes ago!" They had all run as fast as they could to their gate, only to discover that they would have to wait indefinitely.

"Well, that's really messed up! Here we are, trying to get away so we can relax, and look at us now, stuck at the airport!" said Kyle.

"I think someone was already getting very relaxed on this trip," Tab said as she glanced over at Jack.

"Yes, I got some great sleep on that first flight. I haven't had time for a nap like that in months. Which is <u>why</u> we're taking this trip now, to get a break and enjoy it together. Katie, how are you feeling?"

"I'm feeling better now, Dad, thanks," she replied. "I just wish my brother would hold his horses and calm down."

"We know, sweetheart," her mom smiled.

"Ladies and gentlemen, can I have your attention please..." a booming voice came over the speakers. "Fight 273 to Mexico City has been cancelled."

"Cancelled!" Kyle had heard the announcement over the music in his earbuds. "What's going on now?"

"Hush!" Tab shushed him. "What is he saying?"

"...please come to the counter with your tickets. We will issue vouchers for a hotel on site. Shuttles will take you there, and you will all receive priority boarding as soon as we update your itineraries. We apologize for the inconvenience..."

To them it appeared the inclement weather at Houston forced the airline to make the tough call. Even though the Cundiffs and hundreds of other passengers were upset that their schedules changed, they were glad to sleep in fresh beds instead of hard seats.

 Reasons To Travel

They dined that evening in the hotel restaurant. A pianist played quiet tunes on a black grand piano. "I didn't intend to eat at a place this fancy tonight, but here we are!" Jack said. "Let's make the most of this situation."

Lightning flashed outside the windows as the storm continued to roll through the city.

"Why don't we review why we're on this trip?" Jack suggested. "Do you remember the conversations we had last winter? Tab, we'll start with you. Why are you on this trip?"

"Well, after all, it is our *family* vacation! I wanted to travel far away from home, and do it with my husband and kids!"

"I want to take pictures of new places and explore new lands," Katie interjected. "Since we're going to Mexico, I can practice the Spanish that I've learned so far! *¿Hablas español?*"

"How about you, Kyle?"

"I get to be stuck with my old parents and little sister," Kyle said. At 15, he was anxious to get his drivers license, finish school, and move out on his own.

"Well, your frustration with your companions is an honest emotion, son. But what specifically are you looking forward to these next 12 days?"

Kyle stared at his plate for a minute, using his fork to play with his vegetables. His family knew to keep quiet and let him think until he formed his answer. "Maybe I'll find some Mexican girlfriend."

"Woohoo!" Katie cheered.

"Shhhh! That is NOT going to happen!" Tab replied.

"OK, then, um, I'm on this trip to see more of the world than what we have in Maplewood."

"That's fair," Jack replied. "As you all know, my main goal on this trip is to figure out my job situation.

"Over the past few years, in one way or another, you've all said that you wish I'd be home more. Or at least when I am at home, to not be so focused on working. I know that I have neglected you while I prioritized keeping the bills paid and food on the table. But I haven't always been happy in my work, and you've all picked up on that.

"It was a challenge to even plan for all of us to be gone this long on a trip together--we have never been out of town for two weeks. It's new territory for all of us, but as long as we stick together, we'll be fine. We will have to make adjustments as we live among a different culture, and I foresee even more adjustments after we get home."

"Everything will be just fine," Tab reassured her children. She could see in their eyes that they were a little afraid of what may happen. "Did you get enough to eat?"

"Yes," they said.

"I sure did. Maybe we'll treat ourselves to dessert after our stomachs settle a bit. Let's go back to our room," Jack instructed. "Our new flight leaves mid-morning."

They slept fitfully on their unfamiliar mattresses, too excited to rest. They were finally going to Mexico tomorrow!

 Desire For Change

As he dozed, Jack replayed all the events that led up to this trip. He considered their lifestyle, and remembered conversations he had with his wife and kids.

They lived a frantic pace. Tabitha had a daycare in their home each weekday. Jack worked daily for Dan at the hardware store. It seemed like all his other time was spent doing handyman work for people.

Kyle and Katie were both teenagers now, and very involved in school activities. Kyle was in the chess club and played baseball. Katie played trombone in the concert and jazz bands, and was the anchor for the girls' 4 x 100 and 4 x 200 meter relay teams.

Jack and Tabitha continued to teach their popular

family finance class, "A Couple with Common Cents," on the weekends during the school year.

Despite what appeared to be a successful household to the outside world, Jack wanted a recalibration. Many nights before going to sleep, he and Tab brainstormed together what they could do differently.

"We all like to do the things we're involved in right now," Jack had said one of those nights when the full moon beamed through their windows. "However, if we keep up this pace, I'm going to miss our kids' teen years. Before we know it, they'll be moved out!"

"Yes, honey, I know how you feel. You've been telling me off and on for the past two years."

"I'm just not sure what to do about it! What do we change? What can I give up?"

"Maybe we just need to get away for awhile," she said.

"What are you thinking?"

"Jack, we have money saved for a big family vacation. That's the intent of one particular savings account, and we can't just let the thing stockpile forever. Let's use it next summer. We have contacts in ten foreign countries. Why don't we go overseas and visit with one of your old friends? We aren't getting any younger, you know."

"Fly?! I've never flown in a plane. Why do we have to go so far away? Can't we just have an off-site family meeting for an extended weekend somewhere?"

"It's time our kids experienced some other cultures and expanded their horizons beyond small-town America. Sure, we can watch video of people from other places, but there's nothing like going there yourself. Plus, we can encourage the friends that we visit."

"I can't be gone for long. I'm fully booked for five months out, seven if you count for the weather and other delays. Plus, Dan needs me at the hardware store. We're one hand short right now, so all of us are doing extra to make up for that."

"Jack, I've been reading…"

"Oh, what have you read now?"

"I read stories of business people who've taken vacations in order to make decisions on big problems they faced," she said. "Each one of them was surprised as to how long it took before their minds fully disengaged from their home environment."

"How long was that?"

"Those who turned off their electronics, or did not take any with them, or any paperwork or books directly related to their business, took three entire days before their brains and bodies were fully acclimated to their new environment. That means not worrying about work or grabbing their phones just to see what was 'news' every 20 seconds. After one week's time, they were fully enjoying themselves in the new environment and started to get tremendous clarity on the issues they wanted solved."

"A whole *week!*"

"Sure. "And you know what? With all the money in our travel savings, we can be gone for two weeks."

"TWO weeks!"

Jack's blood pressure went up in the hotel room, just like it had in their bedroom those months ago. Then he quietly laughed, because now they were taking the vacation of a lifetime.

 A Boss Who Cares

After breakfast with the family the next morning, Jack checked his phone. He had a voicemail from Dan.

"Jack, Dan here. I see that your flight was cancelled. Hope your family found a place to stay the night."

Jack called him back.

"Thanks for checking in with us, Dan. We're doing great! The airline put us up in a nice hotel, and we just finished breakfast in the restaurant."

"Excellent! I'm glad they are taking care of you."

"Thanks again, sir, for the time off for this family trip. We must get going; they rebooked us for a mid-morning flight."

"Alright, then. Take care, and don't think about

work, OK? We have your duties covered."

"Thanks. I'll call you next week before we head back. Bye."

"Bye Jack."

They re-packed their bags, checked out of the hotel, and flew out of Houston. It was a bright, sunny day.

 Take It All In

"Wow! Look at all that fresh fruit!" Katie exclaimed. Crews of men and women in large brimmed hats were picking oranges in a grove alongside the highway. A large semi-trailer was ready to pull out on the highway, brim full of the orange spheres.

"Are we really going 100 miles an hour?" Kyle asked as he looked at the taxi's dashboard.

"No, Kyle, that's kilometers per hour. It's equal to 62 miles per hour," his mother instructed. "After we get home, look at the small numbers on our car speedometer. It's part of the metric system, which the rest of the world uses."

Suddenly they came upon slow moving traffic.

"Hold on!" Jack cried as the driver slammed on the

brakes. They came to a screeching halt just before hitting the bumper of a silver tin-can minivan.

"We could get whiplash doing that," Kyle blurted out.

"Welcome to Mexico!" the driver smiled through his missing teeth. Jack and Tab laughed nervously. Katie could tell from her mother's expression that this was not a good time to practice her Spanish skills with the driver.

The traffic began to move again. They noticed that the traffic patterns were much different "down here" than back home. Pedestrians, food carts, and animals all shared the road with the motor vehicles. They approached a central square with a beautiful fountain, and several large European-style buildings around the perimeter.

"This...heart of my city," their driver gestured broadly with both hands, then brought them together over his chest. He continued the guided tour in his limited, broken English with extravagant gestures. But the family was busy taking in the exotic sights and sounds around them, and didn't respond very often.

"Wow, this is a beautiful place, Mom! The buildings are so colorful, and the people seem to be so happy!" Katie observed. "Can we stop to get pictures?"

"I think we should just stay in the car until we get to Adrian's house," her father said. "Get a photo or two from here so we'll remember to come back later."

It seemed like it took the entire day to reach their destination.

 Adrian's Family

A *migo!* It's been a long time. Welcome to my home."
Adrian embraced Jack with a big bear hug, then
greeted the rest of the family. "Who is this?"

The teenagers grinned at the sun bronzed muscular
man who had embraced their father.

"Adrian, this is my wife, Tabitha, and our children,
Kyle and Katie."

"Ah, yes, I recognize them from the photo you sent
a few months ago. Welcome, welcome," Adrian shook
their hands. "You look so much better in person! Come
inside, *por favor,* my wife is preparing a meal for you."

"Oh, it's late. We don't need anything to eat right
now…" It was nearly their usual bedtime.

"Please… come… eat… Then we have a place prepared for you to sleep."

"That does smell really good..." Tab caught a whiff of the aroma from the kitchen. "It's making me hungry!" Adrian clapped Jack on the back as they turned and the family followed them into the house. They left their bags in the foyer. Adrian ushered them to seats in the dining room.

"Here is water for everyone."

Two brown skinned boys, just younger than Katie, burst into the room and ran right into their mother. They were talking so fast that Katie could not understand them.

"Ah, this is my family. Jack, this is my wife, Lula, and our two sons, Diego and Miguel." Then he introduced them to his family in their native tongue.

"My boys study English at school. They're shy now, but I'm sure that they will talk to you a lot more in the coming days."

"Aww, they're so cute!" said Katie.

Kyle was checking out the food, trying to figure out what was in the skillet.

"Jack," Adrian asked, "what has happened in your life since we last saw each other?"

"A lot has changed since our high school classes together," Jack replied. "Can you remind me which family you stayed with as an exchange student?"

"Tom and Betty Grey. How are they?"

"They are very old now, doing well for their age, I suppose. Their children all moved out of the state and have families of their own. I haven't seen any of them in years."

"I must write to them. Can you take a letter back with you and personally deliver it for me?"

"Sure, anything for a friend. As for myself, I've worked my whole life at the hardware store in Maplewood. That is, since Tab and I got married 17 years ago. Then we started our family. Kyle is 15 and Katie is 13."

"Growing up fast, aren't they?"

"Yes, they are. I also do a lot of handyman work for other people."

"Handyman? What does that mean?"

"I work with my hands and fix what's broken or I build something new. I can fix plumbing, run new electrical wire, work with wood, put metal together with a welder. You name it, I've probably done it!"

Lula called to her husband.

"The food is ready. I will help my wife bring in your supper," said Adrian.

For the next two hours, they shared the details of their lives as they ate the best tacos the Cundiff family had ever tasted.

 A Morning Conversation

The whole family tossed and turned the entire night. Jack did manage to get some rest, yet it took a while for him to adjust to their sleeping quarters. He woke up the next morning to a rooster crowing in the alley.

As he walked toward the kitchen, Jack smelled a waft of Lula's hot breakfast in the air.

"Good morning!" Adrian called out from the table.

"Buenos dias," Jack said. Both men yawned.

"Is your family up?" asked Adrian.

"They are slowly waking up. Man, this food smells so good. I don't know how you eat like this all the time and look as good as you do."

"Our food is very fresh, my friend. We eat well and get plenty of exercise all day long. There are several shops nearby that supply all the daily needs for our house and food. We don't have to get in a vehicle every day."

"So your neighborhood is built to support a healthy lifestyle."

"Yes, it works out well. My father and his father did the same thing. Even though they traveled to work, they did not have to go far for food."

"Where did they work?"

"My father's father--what's the English word for that?"

"Grandfather."

"Grandfather. Thank you. My grandfather walked a few miles out to his fields and worked the ground to raise crops. My father, who lives close to here, traveled by bus to work in a factory."

"What kind of factory?"

"He made tools out of iron for people to build things. Hammers and screwdrivers, things like that. It was long, hard work. I never saw my father much when I was a kid. My grandfather stayed with us most of the time, until he passed. He was like a father to me.

"I decided that I didn't want to have a job that kept me away from my kids so much. When I say that my family is a priority in my life, my daily activities show that. My boys spell love T-I-M-E. In English, that is!"

Jack laughed for a little bit, then got serious. "Really? You get to spend a lot of time with your kids? How did you pull that off?"

Tabitha walked into the room. Kyle and Katie followed right behind her.

"Are you hungry?" Lula asked.

"Yes," they said.   All eight of them sat down at the table. Both families spent the next several minutes eating their fill.

Adrian was one of the most successful men Jack had ever known. How did he do it? And how did he stay strong as a family man in the midst of his business success? Jack wanted to hear more.

Long Days And
Much Paperwork

Jack persuaded Adrian to take him on a tour. Lula took the rest of the Cundiff family on their own tour around the neighborhood.

"Adrian, tell me more of how you got started. I remember part of the story from years ago, but will you tell me all of it again?"

"Yes. When I finished school, I knew that I only had two options to quickly accomplish my dream of family first: become self-employed, or own a business."

"But you weren't married then. You didn't have kids. You're telling me you planned all of this before you started a family?"

"Yes. Well, sort of, though nothing ever goes *exactly* as planned. Let me explain.

"Because I had just a little cash, I could not go buy shares in a growing company, and I certainly couldn't live off the interest. I started doing odd jobs to grow my savings, providing my services to whoever needed them.

"People loved how hard I worked. Word spread fast about the quality of my work. I was soon working long hours every day and had little time to find a wife. I made good money in those days. But I hit another problem."

"What was that?" Jack asked as they continued walking down a side street.

"There was only one of me, and lots of clients. I raised my prices, and my days stayed full! Raised my prices again, and I couldn't slow down no matter how hard I tried."

"So what did you do?"

"I hired a young man to help me. Hiring someone else was the scariest thing I had done to that point. It scared me worse than drowning in the ocean."

"That's pretty scary."

"Our little service business—handyman is what you called it, I think—took off. A year later I went from one employee to six. It would've been eight, but I had to let two of them go. I made the mistake of hiring two people who just didn't want to do the work."

"Sounds like you were busy."

"Yes, I was very busy. Now I had more paperwork, more people, and I still did a lot of the physical work, too. I had more problems than I even have time to tell you about, Jack. And, I did manage to meet Lula in the middle of all this."

"How did you spend any time with her?"

"I just decided to invest the time in her. I slowly spent less time with clients and more time with her. And I found that my crew got the job done to my standards. They exceeded client expectations, so I didn't have to keep running around 'like a chicken with its head cut off,' as you say in the States."

"Adrian, you know much more English than I realized. How do you know all these words?"

"The simple answer is: my boys and the Internet. I spend time reading and listening every day, and helping my boys learn English. Just because I came back to Mexico after one year in high school with you didn't mean I gave up on my second language. I want to make sure my boys can speak two languages. Most people in the world today are bilingual, you know."

"Actually, I didn't know that."

"Well, here we are! Welcome to the office of *En el Servicio del Rey*, my business."

Adrian opened the door and let Jack inside.

 Delegate And Serve

"Hello!" They were greeted by a lady at the front desk.

"Jack, I want you to meet Alma, my receptionist. Of course she does more than answer the phone and greet me at the door. Alma keeps this office looking sharp and makes sure that we have supplies on hand to get our administrative work done."

Adrian and Jack walked through a hallway with doors on each side.

"In these offices are my bookkeeper, my operations manager, and my marketing director. They're some of my closest friends, and we get a lot of work done together. But we also know when to quit; no one is here at night or on the weekend unless there's an emergency.

Sometimes my crews will work longer days, but that doesn't happen too often."

They entered Adrian's simple, elegant office.

"When do you meet your crews?" Jack asked.

"Once or twice a month I take one or two people from the office and check on the work at each crew site. Sometimes I'll even swing a hammer for an hour. But I never go to a job to boss everyone around. That would be a disaster."

"What do you mean?"

"I have crew managers who are in charge of the men for each project. They have the authority to hire and fire workers. They know how to get things done, and they don't have to come to me or my team for every decision that they need to make. And when I go visit a worksite, I listen to them to see what needs done. I'm not afraid to get my hands dirty. This is how my company has grown so fast, Jack. This whole thing will run without me."

"I thought business owners are supposed to have their hands on everything."

"In a way, I do. Our entire business operates under systems that guide our work. Not just any system, but *efficient* systems. We have a way that we get new clients, a way to fulfill the jobs, a way to run the office, ways to communicate with each other, and a very clear way how to keep track of our data."

"On the surface it seems like there's a lot going on, but now that I really look at this place, you're really organized."

"Thank you, Jack. Yes, we stay organized, but clear organization isn't how I want to be remembered. I want my children and grandchildren to remember me as a man who loved them and really helped them in life, not as some CEO who kept his desk clean. You see, Jack, the point of doing business isn't to have a fancy office or a large bank account. We're here to make the quality of life better for our clients and our families. We do this as servants of the King."

"I know about all this 'serving other people,' but there's some days I want to serve others just to help them out. Sometimes I don't even bill them for my labor."

"Jack, did you see the sign by the entrance?"

"Yes. Why?"

"What did it say?"

"Um, I don't remember. I don't know because I don't read Spanish. Katie can read it."

"The sign is the name of my company: *En el Servicio del Rey.* In English this means: In the Service of the King. We recognize that Jesus is the world's true Lord. He is the King that we serve. We don't work to please Him, for He is already pleased with us because of our faith. We don't work as His slaves, for He has called us friends. No, we work because He has given us domin-ion. We are managers of what He's given to us."

Jack replied, "I thought only those 'in the minis-try' were servants. And I've always regarded Christian service as either something you volunteered to do, you did on staff with a congregation, or you did by raising money to go abroad or do non-profit work. You're tell-ing me that I can serve Jesus in my job?"

"Yes. Why not?"

Jack had no response.

"What is the name of your boss at the hardware store?"

"Dan. Why?"

"How long has he worked there?"

"A long time."

"Do you think that Dan is well-suited for what he does?"

"Sure, he's a great boss, and from what I can tell, he does a fine job running the store."

"Anything else?"

"Dan is a good listener. He's helped me work through tough times in my life. He's a good teacher, too. Kind of like what you're doing right now, asking me all these questions!"

"OK, hang in here with me, Jack. I take the com-parison of me with Dan as a compliment. Do you think it's possible that Dan does his job so well because he's doing what he does best?"

"Sure, that's possible."

"And do you think that Dan can work in other roles and still use his gifts, strengths, and talents?"

"Yes, I think so."

"Have you ever seen Dan, or any of your co-workers, go out of their way to help customers get what they need?"

"Yeah. Where are you going with this?"

Adrian didn't skip a beat. "Wouldn't you say that when you serve someone else, you're putting their needs ahead of your own? And isn't putting other's needs first a way to express love?"

"Yes, I love my wife by helping her do things at home."

"And don't we show our love for God by serving people?"

Jack paused, then said, "Oh, I hadn't thought of it that way before."

"Good. I'll let you think about it some more. Come, Lula will have lunch ready for us in a few minutes."

As they walked out of the office, Jack waved goodbye to Alma.

 Already Pleased

That afternoon, the Cundiff family went sight-seeing together. As they walked through an open air market, Kyle and Katie looked for souvenirs. Katie didn't buy anything yet. She felt like someone was watching her, so she didn't want to get out her money.

Tabitha had an opportunity to talk with Jack out of earshot of the rest of the group. "How was your morning with Adrian?"

"Fine," Jack said.

"What did you talk about?" she prodded.

"His business, how he got started, and what the company is doing now. Adrian's a smart man," he remarked, "not because of his education or his abilities, but because he's designed his business around his family, not the other way around."

Tabitha wanted to hear more. "Honey, what's one thing you learned this morning that we can use in our life?"

"Let me think on that for a bit."

They walked past vendors selling beautiful hand-made jewelry, plaster figurines, and bright colored clothing.

"I guess the main thing I learned is that in my work, I need to charge clients full price and not devalue my skills. And all of it, no matter what I do, whether it's repairs on a client's home, helping a customer at the hardware store, or doing the dishes for you, is all service to Jesus, because I'm serving people."

"Jack, that reminds me of a book I read recently. We know Jesus as divine. But it reminded me that we can't forget His human side. Between the ages of 12 and 30, He worked alongside Joseph, his earthly father, learning a trade. As the oldest son, when Joseph died, Jesus was responsible for taking care of the family. Jack, Jesus was a blue-collar worker!"

"I remember He was a carpenter, but haven't really thought about it."

"Jack, Jesus was more than a carpenter. He worked with stone and wood. He didn't go study to become a scribe, or be trained as a rabbi. Instead, He was part of the working class. Jesus made work a holy thing!"

"Yeah, Paul said, 'Whatever you eat or drink, or whatever you do, do all to the glory of God.' That has encouraged me in the past, and today's discussions with you and Adrian have encouraged me more. I've always felt guilty that I wasn't 'doing enough' to serve God. But now I realize I can't ever 'do enough' for He is already pleased with me."

Jack's eyes lit up and his grin covered his face from ear to ear. He was so excited!

"Tab, I can't ever earn more of His love. He's already given me everything!" Jack threw up his arms and laughed out loud.

Soon he realized that all the vendors and shoppers within 100 feet were looking at him like he was a crazy man!

"Oh sorry, I got a little carried away," he said to everyone, as if they could understand him.

"Honey, there's no need to apologize. You have a good reason to be excited. What you're learning is bringing you more freedom. Why not have a celebration?"

Just then, a pickpocket took advantage of the distraction and bumped into Katie. He quickly cut the strap and snatched her purse.

"Hey, watch it there!" she said, not realizing what had just happened.

But Jack had seen the whole thing.

"Hey! Stop, you thief!"

The mugger realized he was caught, and dodged through the crowd, hoping to get away. Jack immediately sprinted after him.

Mayhem In
The Marketplace

The purse snatcher was fast, and it was obvious that he knew the area well. He bolted down alleys and around corners without hesitation. As Jack chased him through the market, they turned over tables, knocking down displays. Goods and money flew up in the air, then crashed to the ground behind them as they ran. A few vendors even got knocked down! They really made a mess of things.

Jack was getting short of breath, but he continued the chase. The thief finally threw down Katie's purse. Jack stopped to pick it up and catch his breath. The pickpocket had vanished; he was nowhere to be seen.

Tabitha and the kids were in shock over the ordeal and had stayed put where they were. This made it easy for Jack to find them, though it took him a few minutes to get back there.

Tab spotted Jack coming up the street and ran to meet him. "Honey, are you OK? Did you catch that man?"

"I'm fine. No, I didn't catch him," he took a deep breath, "but here's Katie's stuff."

"Did you get everything, Dad?" Katie walked up to her parents and retrieved her damaged purse.

"The thief just gave up and threw it on the ground when he realized I wasn't going to quit chasing him. I thought he might turn around on me and pull a knife, but he just vanished into thin air."

"My camera has a few scratches on it, but still works, and the memory card is still here. That's good," Katie said as she examined her belongings. "I think he was after my money, Dad. All that's left are small bills."

"How much did you have on you?" Kyle asked.

"I had dollars and pesos in my purse," she replied. "All of the dollars are gone, and the large pesos are gone. He took close to 100 bucks."

"Ouch," Kyle winced. "Guess you're not buying any souvenirs!"

Katie started to sob. "What do I do now, Mom?"

"Lets get back to Adrian's house and call it a day, shall we?" Tab put an arm around her and handed her a tissue.

The Cundiffs walked out to the street, found a cab, and went back to the house. After a few minutes of quiet they were able to take a nap. Everyone, that is, except Katie. She got out her journal and began writing about the events that had transpired since they left home.

 Las Estacas

"Let's go out to the countryside. I will show you more of beautiful Mexico," Adrian suggested the next morning at breakfast. "You, Jack, are still in work mode. We need to take a vacation from your vacation so your mind can slow down!"

"Where do you want to take us?" Tab asked.

"I know of a few places we can go, about a half-day drive from here, that will get you up-close with the wild outdoors."

"Are there snakes?" Kyle asked.

"Spiders?" asked Katie.

"Yes, snakes and spiders. And they're all poisonous, just waiting for some tasty children to walk near enough to bite them!" Adrian leaped out of his chair toward them. Katie let out a yell, Kyle jumped, but Diego and Miguel just laughed.

"He likes to have fun, if you couldn't tell," said Lula.

"Are all eight of us going?" asked Jack.

"Why not? We will prepare some food and gather supplies this morning, and then leave after lunch. Is that OK?"

"Sure," they said.

Except for a flat tire, this day went smoothly. They pulled into the camping spot at Las Estacas just before dusk. When they stepped out of the van, they were surrounded by tropical trees, running water, and colorful birds that the Cundiffs had never seen before.

"Wow, this place is great!" said Tabitha.

Both families worked together to set up their campsites. Lula and Tabitha focused on preparing supper.

After his tent was up, Kyle walked to the nearest restroom. When he came out, a Mexican girl caught his eye. She glanced at him and giggled.

Kyle followed this beautiful female to a water hole where several people were swimming.

 English Class

F ood's almost ready," said Tab.
"Where's Kyle?" asked Jack.

"The last time I saw him, he was going to the restroom," said Katie.

"I hope he's not having problems in there!" said Jack. "Adrian, would you help me look for my son? Bring a flashlight. Everyone else stay here. If we're not back in 15 minutes, Tab, go ahead and eat."

Jack and Adrian checked the nearest set of restrooms. "Kyle, are you in here? It's time to eat."

They heard nothing, and went to the next set of restrooms. "Kyle, it's dad. Are you in here?" Silence. "It's time to eat!" Still nothing.

As they walked toward the next set, Adrian suddenly stopped to listen. "I hear two voices that I recognize, in that direction," he said as he pointed toward the edge of the campground.

"Should we check it out?" asked Jack.

"Yes. But not too fast."

As Jack and Adrian approached the water, Jack recognized Kyle. He was sitting at the edge of the lake, having a simple conversation in English—with a girl!

"Kyle! What are you doing over here?" asked Jack.

When Jack said "Kyle!" the girl turned to look at him. She immediately jumped in the water and swam away into the night.

Kyle didn't know what to think. First, his dad caught him talking to a girl. Second, she fled the scene before he could get her name or contact info.

"Kyle!"

Kyle stood up. "I was just talking with this girl because she wanted to practice her English and…"

"Well, English class is over. It's time to eat."

Adrian wanted to laugh, but he stifled it.

"What was our first rule for this trip?" asked Jack.

"Always tell someone else where you're going if you go somewhere by yourself," said Kyle as he looked at the ground.

"Did you do that?"

"I just needed to go to the restroom, which was within eyeshot of our campsite, and then when I came out I…"

"Did you tell us where you were going?" Jack asked again.

"No."

Please hand me your phone."

"What?"

"Yes, Kyle, please give me your phone. You'll get it back when we pull into the driveway at home."

"Are you serious? We were just talking!"

"I'm not upset that you were polite and respectful with that girl. I'm not judging your motives. However, you did leave the group for at least half an hour without telling anyone where you were going. Plus, it's time for you to enjoy the scenery instead of playing some game or texting your friends. Learn to enjoy each moment when you're down here."

Kyle slowly handed his phone to his dad. "It only had five percent battery left, anyway."

They rejoined the rest of the group and ate another delicious supper together. By the time everyone finished their campfire stories, Kyle had forgotten about his phone. But he sure hadn't forgotten about the brown eyes he had talked with earlier in the evening.

 Awkward Breakfast

W ake up, Kyle. I want to introduce you to someone!" Adrian called the next morning. Kyle was
the last one out of his tent; all the others were ready for
the day, with breakfast on the way.

Kyle looked out the window of the tent. The girl he
had met last night was talking with Adrian and Lula!

Oh no, am I in trouble again? he wondered. He was
nervous but still managed to get dressed for the day.

Kyle unzipped his tent and walked out, blushing.

"Kyle, I want you to meet my niece, Belen! She
works here at the campgrounds."

"Um, we've, uh, already met," he stammered.

"Yes, that's what she tells me."

"Oh, Kyle's got a girlfriend!" Katie teased.

"My niece says that you helped her practice speaking English last night. She said that she is a little rusty in her foreign languages."

"How old are you?" Tab asked his niece.

"Nineteen."

"Nineteen! Kyle, she's way too old for you! You don't even have a license yet."

Everyone but Kyle and Belen let out a big laugh. Adrian translated for his niece.

"How old…are you?" she asked Kyle.

"Fifteen."

She said something in Spanish. "She says you're quite a gentleman for 15 years old. You're not like the other boys she knows who are 15." Adrian translated for the Cundiffs.

"Breakfast is ready," said both of Adrian's boys. They invited their cousin to join them.

Kyle and Belen exchanged quick glances as they ate.

Well, after that awkward introduction, this is not so bad, Kyle thought.

 Missing Document

The Cundiff and Sanchez families stayed at the park for a few more days. Adrian's niece continued to visit their campsite for meals. Her English speaking skills noticeably improved. Kyle and Katie gained more Spanish and Diego and Miguel had fun with their cross-cultural conversations as well.

Then they left Las Estacas. Adrian took them to see a few famous historical sites. They took photos at the base of tribal pyramids and drove past an active volcano.

"There's smoke coming out of that volcano," said Tab. "Will it erupt while we're here?"

"No worries. That thing has smoked for a long time. If it does release anything else, we'll be far enough away that we won't get hurt."

As the volcano disappeared into the horizon behind them, Katie started to search through her purse. "I know it's in here somewhere."

"What?" said Kyle.

She dumped all the contents of her purse into her lap. "Where is it?"

"Where is what, honey?" asked her mother.

"I can't find my passport."

"You can't find your *passport?*" Kyle was incredulous.

Katie was getting frustrated. "I know I had it in here!"

"When was the last time you saw it?" asked Jack.

"I had it in the airport when we went through customs."

"Obviously," said Kyle sarcastically.

"Take your time and think," Her father advised. "When did you last see your passport in your purse?"

"I don't know…" Katie started to cry. "Now I'll be stuck down here forever because I can't get back home!"

"That wouldn't be so bad," Adrian teased. "I would enjoy having a daughter! We'd take care of you!"

"Yeah, that wouldn't be bad at all!" Kyle laughed.

"Oh, come here," said Tab as she put her arms around her daughter. "We will go through all of our stuff as soon as we get back to Adrian and Lula's house. That goes for everybody. We all need to make sure we have our passports. We fly home in three days!"

Katie was still worried that it was lost. She wanted to get back quickly to search the rest of her stuff.

 Frantic Search

When Adrian pulled the van up to the house, Katie flew to her suitcase. She tossed every item out, searching for her passport. Every compartment was opened as she tore through all her belongings. The rest of the family had watched from the doorway.

But the passport was not there. She sat down on the floor in defeat.

"I bet I know where it is," Katie mumbled through gritted teeth.

"It wasn't me," Kyle threw up his hands defensively.

"I'm not blaming you. It was that thief in the market!"

"The thief took it?" said Jack. "I thought all he got

was cash."

"Well, apparently he stole my passport, too."

After a careful search of all their luggage (and the entire house), Tabitha asked Adrian if she could use his computer.

"Sure!" he quickly logged in and helped her insert a thumb drive in the USB port.

"Come here, Katie," Tab called her daughter to the computer. "Take your eyes off the floor and look at the screen."

"That's my passport front page!" said Katie. "How'd you get that?"

"Mom is always prepared! Before we left home, I made scans of all our passports. I can just print this out, take it, and you, and some other paperwork to the American Embassy. They should be able to issue you a new one!"

"Really?"

"Yes," Jack added. "And we'll have to pay something, too. But don't worry about it, Katie. Adrian, let's call the American Embassy to find out their hours and verify the process to issue a new passport."

"Got it," said Adrian.

"Way to go, Tab!" Jack gave her a high five. "I knew you were well organized,"

"Just doing what I do best, honey," she replied smugly as she gave Katie a hug.

 Play To Your Strengths

The next morning, Lula took Tabitha and Katie to the embassy the moment it opened. Jack decided to tag along with Adrian again while Kyle stayed back to play soccer with Diego and Miguel.

Jack was deep in thought as he walked with Adrian to the headquarters of *En el Servicio del Rey*.

Just doing what I do best. Jack couldn't stop thinking about what Tab had said yesterday. *When have I heard that before?*

Just doing what I do best, Jack. Quick, we want to make sure we catch our connection. Tab said that at the airport on our way down here.

Do you think it's possible that Dan does his job so well because he's doing what he does best? Adrian said this the other day in his office.

"That's it!" Jack yelled. He startled Adrian as the others on the street looked at him.

"What is it?" Adrian asked.

Jack was excited. "That's it! I've figured out the next piece of my puzzle."

"How's that?"

"I kept hearing Tabitha say in my head, 'Just doing what I do best.' And she's right! That's what I should focus on—what I do best. When I'm doing tasks that I like to do, that I forget about the passing of time, and that I'm compensated well for, then I've hit my groove!"

"'Hit your groove'? What do you mean?"

"When I hit my groove is when I'm doing work that is well-suited for me *and* that commands premium prices. I'm not a commodity, Adrian!"

"You're right," he replied as they walked in the front door.

After they greeted the employees in the office, Jack sat down near Adrian's desk. Adrian shut the door.

"So then, what is it that you do best?"

Jack rattled off a list as Adrian wrote them down on a piece of paper:

- Diagnose engine problems
- Fix cars

- Help customers find their desired items quickly at the hardware store
- Plumbing
- Electrical
- Woodworking
- Teach other families how to manage money well

"Ok. Jack, you have a list here that ranges all the way from retail sales to household services to adult education."

"Yeah, it's quite a diverse list. I think I'm good at all of them."

"I know you're good at many things," said Adrian. "You've demonstrated that well during your stay with us. What on this list do you hate doing? As in, if you didn't have to do any of these things, what would you cross off?"

"Oh, that's easy. Plumbing. Nothing against plumbers, but I just hate crawling under sinks and crawlspaces to fix pipes."

"Good. We'll cross that one off. Anything else?"

"Sometimes it's boring at the hardware store when no customers come in for an hour or two. I like helping people, and I know where everything is on the store floor, but it's boring at times. But I can't just walk away from it—I'd miss Dan and my coworkers. I can't even think about leaving that place; I've been there so long!"

"I'm not asking you to quit anything at the moment, Jack. I'm just helping you see what tasks you can give up. What else on this list do you hate?"

"Well, we need to add something else to the list so we can scratch it off!"

"What's that?"

"Sales and marketing. I have the hardest time promoting myself. Most of my business has come from word-of-mouth and conversations while at the hardware store. It's like the store and my handyman work have gone hand-in-hand."

"That's excellent that you recognize that about yourself, Jack. You really are thinking things through."

"I might be thinking so clearly today because my mind had an extended break and I wasn't focused on my issues while camping."

"I bet you're right. I knew our camping trip would help. Now, pick one more thing from your list to cross off."

"Um, let's see…electrical work. There's all kinds of regulations with that. I know code, but when you're dealing with old woven wire in houses over 60 years old, it can be a pain."

Here's the list they had now:

- Diagnose engine problems
- Fix cars
- Help customers find their desired items quickly at the hardware store
- ~~Plumbing~~
- ~~Electrical~~
- Woodworking
- Teach other families how to manage money well
- ~~Sales and marketing~~

Jack looked at the list. "Now wait, if there's no sales, how can I stay in business?"

"Maybe someone else can do that for you."

"I can't afford a sales person! How am I supposed to bring them on staff?"

"I didn't say that you need to hire an employee to do that."

"Well, it's my business and I don't want someone else selling for me."

"Jack, didn't you tell me before that your wife did your paperwork for you?"

"Yes. Why?"

"Would you consider Tabitha your administrative assistant? Isn't she your accountant and bookkeeper?"

"Yeah, she's good with math."

"Then you're not a one-man show at the moment,

are you?"

"She's my wife. It's a one man and woman show."

"Then why would it be any different to have a second person help you if you already have one?"

"I want to keep this a family-run thing. Plus, I don't have the time to look after someone else."

"Do you? Would a part-time sales guy on commission really cost you more, or would he free up more of your time?"

"I told you, I don't need a sales guy!"

 The Jack Of All Trades

Jack, are you just so stubborn that you want to be a solo entrepreneur? The super husband who wants to prove to someone (I don't know who), that he can do all this by himself?"

Jack stood up, angry. He was about to walk out on Adrian.

But then his words went from Jack's head to his heart. Deep down, he knew there was truth to what Adrian was saying. He recognized that his friend wanted to help him.

Jack turned around to face Adrian and slowly made his way back to his seat. "You're right," he admitted. "I am stubborn."

Adrian knew Jack needed a minute to cool off.

"Let me give you a short history lesson. It has to do with your name and current situation. Do you know about the origin of the phrase 'the jack of all trades'?"

"Yeah, 'and master of none' is how it goes," Jack replied.

"No, actually it didn't start out that way. 'Jack of all trades' was originally used in English as a positive description of a person. It was a term of praise."

"Really?"

"Yes."

"I don't believe it."

"Jack, isn't it a compliment to be competent in many endeavors?"

"Sure if 'master of none' wasn't implied."

"Is that because you don't know anyone else like this?"

"Wow, Adrian, your questions always dig deep to the heart of the matter. I don't know very many people like me."

"Well, that makes you unique, right?"

"Yes, each one of us is unique. Now that I think about it, I do know a guy who does well at everything he sets out to do. He can play several musical instruments, give speeches, take outstanding photos, speak three or four languages, is in great physical shape, teaches in a non-native language, and has a family. Jon is so smart."

"OK, hold that thought. You said 'languages' which reminded me of a phrase we have in Spanish:

"A todo le tiras, y a nada le pegas.

"This means 'You shoot at everything, and hit nothing.'"

"I like that."

"Here's another one:

"Quien mucho abarca poco aprieta.

"This means, 'Don't bite off more than you can chew.'"

"That's funny," said Jack. "But I don't think my friend Jon aimed to do all of what he does at once. He's learned new things over the years and just keeps adding to his skills."

"Exactly. Jon didn't get there overnight."

There was a knock at the door. It was his receptionist, Alma. She spoke quickly with Adrian.

"What was that?"

"Jack, come with me. I'm going to introduce you to a work crew."

 Seasons Of Learning

The men walked back to the house to get the van. They continued their conversation.

"Jack, do you think Jon has mastered everything he's ever done?"

"I doubt it. But he is good at what he does."

"I bet if you were to ask him, he took a season of his life to focus on a few things. Then in the next season, added to his skill set while continuing to practice what he already knew. And I'd also bet that he's had to let a few skills go over the years as he finds less and less use of them."

"I bet you're right," said Jack.

"I need to go in the house for a few minutes. Wait for me right here, and then I'll drive you to the worksite," said Adrian.

While Adrian was away, Jack powered up his phone. He found a wireless network so he decided to give Dan a quick call via the data connection.

"Hi Dan, Jack here."

"Hey Jack! Good to hear your voice. How is Mexico?"

"We're doing well overall, and having a great trip. At this moment Katie is getting a duplicate passport because hers was stolen while we were shopping in the open market."

"That's not good."

"It will be OK. They're getting it taken care of right now. I'm spending time with Adrian and have learned a lot about how he does business."

"Great! You can share everything after you get back. Got to go, there's a call on the other line. See you soon!"

"Bye."

Adrian returned, and the boys joined them.

"What's up now? Can we go with you?"

"Sure," said Adrian. "*¡Vamos!*"

Kyle, Diego, and Miguel piled into the back of the van. Jack rode up front with Adrian.

"Hold on," said Adrian. "I might drive a little different since the women aren't with us!" He gave Jack a wink.

Centuries Of
Renaissance Men

Two minutes later, Jack was having flashbacks from their first Mexican taxi ride! Adrian wove in and out of traffic wherever he found an open spot. The boys were having a great time!

"It's almost like a river," Jack observed. "You just go with the traffic flow."

"Biggest vehicle has the right-of-way," said Adrian. "And this van might be little to you, but we're bigger than most everyone else out here!"

"I won't need to go to an amusement park for another five years," Jack decided. The reckless driving (by American standards, anyway) had made the trip feel like hours.

"Here we are!" said Adrian.

The construction crew was busy working on a new, large building. The crew chief met them and exchanged greetings with Adrian.

"Jack, this is Rodrigo. He only speaks Spanish, so if you have questions, I'll translate for you." Jack and Rodrigo shook hands.

The men and boys donned gloves and hard hats as they followed Rodrigo into the building.

"You're almost done with this, aren't you?" Jack observed as he examined the building. "Ask Rodrigo how much longer before they finish."

"Two months," Adrian said after translation.

"What will this building be when it's done?" asked Kyle.

"Yeah, it's not an apartment or an office building," said Jack.

They stopped for Adrian to translate the question, and hear the answer.

"Rodrigo said that it's a new museum. It will display the history of science, math, exploration, art, and music."

"That's quite a variety of subjects for one museum," Jack said. Adrian interpreted.

"Yes, these fields don't appear to be connected," was Rodrigo's reply. "But ten men with ties to Mexico City who lived from the 1400's to today, had achievements in those areas that will be honored here."

"Fascinating. I wonder who these ten men are?" asked Kyle.

"The museum curators won't tell us. We can only guess," Rodrigo replied through Adrian's translation, "that most of them are from the Renaissance period. In fact, that's what we call them, 'Renaissance men'."

"Kind of like Jon," said Jack.

Adrian took a few minutes to fill in Rodrigo on Jon and the types of conversations he's had with Jack.

"Ah," said Rodrigo. *"Mil usos."* Diego and Miguel laughed.

"What's that mean?" asked Kyle.

"One thousand jobs," said Diego. "It means, you have to do everything, and because of that, you really don't become really good at any of them."

"That's how I feel some days," Jack laughed ruefully.

"Listen," Rodrigo said through Adrian, "My friend and I know enough about everything it takes to build this building. We could do it on our own. Or, could we? If we tried, just him, just me, or the two of us, it would take many, many years. It would only be one story tall, too.

"Would it look OK? Maybe. Would the water run and not leak? Yes. Would all the lights and computers work? Sure.

"But there's lots of other people who can do many

of these jobs better than us, and they can do it quicker, too. Plus, look at how tall this building is. One man can't do this by himself.

"Look at how many families we help by providing ample wages and the dignity of pride in their work to the crew. Years from now, hundreds of grandchildren will hear their grandfathers say, 'Look at what I helped build.'

"We specialize in our tasks so that the entire job is done better. Renaissance men still exist today, but not everyone will be like Jon. And that's OK. Don't compare yourself to everyone else, Jack. Be the best you."

"You've taught your sons and workers well," said Jack.

"Thank you," replied Adrian. "Let's look over their work. Rodrigo and I have some business to do while I'm here. Come, we'll go this way."

The group spent the afternoon admiring the details of craftsmanship and watching the men work diligently. Adrian and Rodrigo took some time apart to consult about the project. The others passed out bottled water to the workers during their short siesta break.

Adrian's phone rang. "The women are on their way home," he said. "They must have found favor at the embassy. We should go."

Jack and Kyle said their good-byes to the crew and to Rodrigo. Before they left, Adrian grabbed a quick photo of all of them standing in front of the new museum.

 Before The Trip Ends

I have a new passport!" Katie met her father at the van. "They're printing it right now."

"Jack, we have to pick up her passport on the way to the airport on Thursday. They should have it done before our departure," Tab said.

"Should?"

"We paid for expedited processing, which will get the new passport in her hands about two hours before takeoff."

"Wow, that's cutting it close!"

"Well, it was a lot cheaper doing it that way than calling the airline to change all our tickets for a week from now."

"Good thinking, Tab."

They gathered with cold drinks in the kitchen.

"You leave in two days. Less than that, actually. What else do you want to see or do before you leave?"

"I would like to see your niece again…" Kyle interjected quickly.

"Sure, just to help her with her English!" teased Katie. Diego and Miguel laughed.

"I don't think you can see her, but I might be able to catch her on the phone. Anyone else? Tabitha?"

"I wouldn't know what else to do. I've had a good trip. Let the others decide. Katie?"

"I would like to return to the city square and get those pictures we missed on our taxi ride coming here," Katie replied.

"Yes," agreed Jack. "And I'd like the three of you to see Adrian's office. We could get a family photo there as well."

"Excellent! Let's go to the square for dinner tonight. Tomorrow the rest of you can tour my office. Then you can pack tomorrow night, so you're ready to go to the embassy first thing," said Adrian.

"Sounds like a plan!" said Tabitha.

After an hour of rest, they went to a night market near the square. Katie took lots of photos. For dinner, they sampled the local street vendors' fare.

 It's Gone

At the airport on Thursday, the Cundiff and Sanchez families quickly said their good-byes. "Now, last check. Everyone have their luggage and passports?" Tabitha asked.

"Yes," Kyle and Katie responded.

"I don't have my ticket," said Jack.

"*I* have all our tickets!" Tab announced. "Let's go!"

At the ticket counter, the airline representative said, "You're just in time to check in for your flight. You'll need to get through customs quickly; I don't want you to miss your plane!"

"Thank you," said Jack.

The Cundiffs jogged up to the customs line. They cleared customs and ran to their gate, arriving just as first class was boarding. They took their seats on the plane.

"Now we can relax," breathed Tabitha.

"I was already relaxed," Jack smiled at his wife.

"Can I have my phone back now? This is a long flight," Kyle pleaded.

"You'll get it back when we get home tonight," replied his father.

That evening, when the Cundiffs were driving just a few miles from home, Jack spotted a red glow in the dark horizon.

"Honey do you see that?"

"What is it, Jack?"

"That red glow. Is that a fire?"

"Hmm. Do you think we should check it out?"

"Katie, get your camera ready. You may be a photojournalist tonight. Kyle, here is your phone. We're going to check this out before we go home."

They drove past their own street toward the center of town.

"Jack, it looks like half the town is in flames!"

A fire truck rushed past them. Another fire engine came up quickly behind them, so Jack just pulled the car over into a parking spot.

"Let's get out here," he said.

As they turned the corner, Tabitha grabbed Jack's arm.

"Oh, no…" she moaned.

They all stopped on the sidewalk, speechless. The entire east side of the town square was in flames.

The hardware store was gone.

 An Unusual Meeting

The next morning at ten o'clock Dan held a meeting at his house for all employees of the hardware store.

"Thank you for coming," Dan said as he began his remarks. "Last night is a night that we will always remember. Though we've lost a landmark that is near and dear to each of our hearts, I have not lost any of you, thank God. No one was hurt in last night's fire.

"The police and firemen are conducting an investigation at this moment to determine the cause of the fire. I'm not going to assume or suggest the cause until after they've spoken with me. I'll tell the press the same thing at 11:30 that I'm telling you right now. But I wanted to let all of you know first, in person.

"Neither my wife nor I could sleep much last night. From the looks of your faces, I don't think many of you did, either." Nervous laughter came from some of the group.

"What will happen now?" one of them asked.

"The first thing is to wait a while before going forward," Dan replied. "I don't want emotion to cloud sound judgment. My wife and I have a few options from prior planning we did, in the event that something like this would happen. In order to keep from putting off this important decision, we've set a deadline of two weeks from today to consider all our options, consult with each of you, and make sure we're doing what is right for us as a group. And as for your pay, each one of you will receive your normal pay for the next fourteen days."

The employees gave a standing ovation to Dan's generosity and determined wisdom that he had just shown them. Jack gave Dan a big smile as he joined the applause of his coworkers.

 Reorganization

A week later, Dan came to see Jack privately.
"Now that you've had a week to rest from your trip and time to consider your options, what's on your mind?" Dan asked Jack.

"I sure didn't expect things to turn out like this when we got home," Jack replied.

"None of us did. Tell me, what do you want to do?"

"I need to focus, that's for sure."

Jack told Dan the details of their trip and all that he learned from Adrian.

"Adrian gave you some great advice," Dan said. "Now, let me share something with you. I've spoken with several other retail businesses in a 30-mile radius, and a few are hiring right now. Some of my employees will take those jobs.

"But some of them are very loyal to me, and don't want to go anywhere else. They want me to reopen the hardware store.

"My wife and I have agreed that the hardware store had a good run. Given the projections we made at the beginning of this year, and looking at what our town really needs right now, we think it's best not to reopen."

"Oh, wow," Jack exclaimed. He paused for a moment to consider what all this meant.

"Jack, you are well respected by your coworkers. You've been dedicated and loyal, you know how to get things done, and you're good with people. I have considered all of that, and your desire to spend more time with your family, and your new perspective since Mexico.

"And I wondered... Would you consider letting me help *you* in your business venture?"

"You help *me?*" asked Jack. "I don't know what to say. I mean, what would that look like?"

"Here's an idea. It's just an idea, but let's get it on the table. You will focus on what you do best and what you like to do (we all will). You're the founder, of course, and you already have Tabitha keeping the books. Right?"

"Right."

"So let's say I come in as your operations manager, or COO. I'd take care of the administrative stuff, work on the marketing plan, and oversee systems and staff."

"Staff?"

"Sure. I know of at least two people, possible three, that can help. One is great as an assistant, another is really good at sales. The third is like you; he works with his hands. We can outsource all the rest. What do you say?"

"I'd have to discuss this with Tabitha first."

"Of course. I expect you to run it by her. Compile all your ideas and questions on paper, and we'll meet about it on Monday. That gives you three days before we hash it out again."

"Thank you so much, Dan. I wish there were more people like you and Adrian."

"I do, too."

 Master Of One

One year later, Jack attended an afternoon baseball game with Tabitha. "Look at our son playing out there at shortstop. Doesn't he look great?" said Tab.

"Yes, he does. And I'm so glad that I can watch the game in person and show him my support. Thanks to help from Adrian and Dan, I can take off work every afternoon and not be chained to the phone if I want!"

The batter hit the ball a little short of left field. Kyle picked it off the ground, threw it to second, then the ball went to first.

Jack was on his feet. "Double play!" he yelled.

"That's my son out there!" he said to the neighboring fans as they were all on their feet.

"Mom, check out these pictures I took of Kyle just

now!" Katie said.

"Your skills keep getting better every day! Those look great," her mother replied.

"Those are so good you should sell them. Hey, how about I talk to the coach and the newspaper editor tomorrow? Maybe they'd pay you for your best prints," Jack said.

"I'd pay for pictures of my grandson," said a lady sitting behind them. "I don't mean to interrupt, but he's the one out there in right field. He graduates next year, and I'd like to give him my scrapbook of his activities as his graduation present."

"Well, let's make a deal then. This is my daughter, Katie. I'm Jack, and this is Tabitha. How many and what type of photos do you want?"

"Oh, Jack," said Tabitha, laughing.

"Just helping my daughter earn some money from what she does best!"

ACKNOWLEDGMENTS

A book always requires the support of many people to get it done. Thank you to my wife, Lori, for giving me time to write. Thank you to Susan White for your editorial and layout expertise.

The words of many other authors inspired the ideas in this story. I give a special mention to Chris Shoemaker, Perry Marshall, Sam Carpenter, Dan Miller, Michael Hyatt, Jeff Goins, and Dave Ramsey for shaping my views about small business and entrepreneurship. Thank you also to Adrian S., Lula S., and Micaela S. for proofreading the Spanish text in this book.

Thank you to Jesus Christ, Who shows us patience as we discover our gifts. You alone show us the best way to serve others, and it is You who provides for our every need—and so much more.

NOTES

Delegate and Serve
Systems that guide our work: See the book *Work the System.*
He is already pleased with us: Hebrews 11:6
He has called us friends: John 15:15
We are managers of what He's given to us: Matthew 25:14ff
Already Pleased
Jesus was a blue-collar worker...He worked with stone and wood...made work a holy thing: See the book *Jesus: A Theography,* p. 97 and p. 100.
Whatever you eat or drink, or whatever you do, do all to the glory of God: 1 Corinthians 10:31
He's already given us everything: Ephesians 1:3

FOR FURTHER READING

To explore the ideas in *The Jack of One Trade* further, read these books. (A citation does not imply endorsement of everything these authors teach.)

Buckingham, Marcus. *StandOut: The Groundbreaking New Strengths Assessment from the Leader of the Strengths Revolution.* Nashville: Thomas Nelson, 2011.

Carpenter, Sam. *Work the System: The Simple Mechanics of Making More and Working Less, Third Edition.* Austin, TX: Greenleaf Book Group Press, 2012.

Cloud, Henry. *The Power of the Other: The Startling Effect Other People Have on You, from the Boardroom to the Bedroom and Beyond—and What to Do About It.* New York: Harper Business, 2016.

Crawford, Matthew B. *Shop Class as Soulcraft: An*

Inquiry into the Value of Work. New York: Penguin, 2009.

Franklin, Benjamin. *The Autobiography of Benjamin Franklin, Second Edition.* New Haven, CT: Yale University Press, 1964.

Gerber, Michael E. *Awakening the Entrepreneur Within: How Ordinary People Can Create Extraordinary Companies.* New York: Collins, 2008.

Godin, Seth. *Linchpin: Are You Indispensable?* New York: Portfolio, 2010.

____. *The Dip: A Little Book that Teaches You When to Quit (And When to Stick).* New York: Portfolio, 2007.

Goins, Jeff. *The Art of Work: A Proven Path to Discovering What You Were Meant to Do.* Nashville: Nelson Books, 2015.

Guillebeau, Chris. *Born For This: How to Find the Work You Were Meant to Do.* New York: Crown Business, 2016.

Gwartney, James, Richard L. Stroup, and Dwight R. Lee. *Common Sense Economics: What Everyone Should Know About Wealth and Prosperity.* New York: St. Martin's Press, 2005.

Henry, Todd. *Die Empty: Unleash Your Best Work Every Day.* New York: The Penguin Group, 2013.

Hyatt, Michael. *Your Best Year Ever: A 5-Step Plan for Achieving Your Most Important Goals.* Grand Rapids,

MI: Baker Books, 2018.

Hyatt, Michael and Daniel Harkavy. *Living Forward: A Proven Plan to Stop Drifting and Get the Life You Want.* Grand Rapids, MI: Baker Books, 2016.

Koch, Richard. *The Natural Laws of Business: How to Harness the Power of Evolution, Physics, and Economics to Achieve Business Success.* New York: Doubleday, 2001.

Lospennato, Leonardo. *The Da Vinci Curse: Life design for people with too many interests and talents.* Berlin: Umlaut Publishing, 2012.

Marshall, Perry. *80/20 Sales and Marketing: The Definitive Guide to Working Less and Making More.* Berkley, CA: Entrepreneur Press, 2013.

Miller, Dan. *No More Dreaded Mondays: Ignite Your Passion—And Other Revolutionary Ways to Discover Your True Calling at Work.* New York: Broadway Books, 2008.

Miller, Dan and Jared Angaza. *Wisdom Meets Passion: When Generations Collide and Collaborate.* Nashville: Thomas Nelson, 2012.

Ramsey, Dave. *EntreLeadership: 20 Years of Practical Business Wisdom from the Trenches.* New York: Howard Books, 2011.

Sanders, Tim. *Today We Are Rich: Harnessing the Power of Total Confidence.* Carol Stream, IL: Tyndale House Publishers, Inc., 2011.

Sinek, Simon. *Find Your Why: A Practical Guide for Discovering Purpose for You and Your Team.* New York: Portfolio / Penguin, 2017.

Slim, Pamela. *Body of Work: Finding the Thread That Ties Your Story Together.* New York: The Penguin Group, 2013.

Smith, Robert D. *20,000 Days and Counting: The Crash Course for Mastering Your Life Right Now.* Nashville: Thomas Nelson, 2012.

Streznewski, Marylou Kelly. *Gifted Grownups: The Mixed Blessings of Extraordinary Potential.* New York: John Wiley & Sons, 1999.

Sweet, Leonard and Frank Viola. *Jesus: A Theography.* Nashville: Thomas Nelson, 2012.

Welch, Jack and Suzy Welch. *The Real-Life MBA: Your No-BS Guide to Winning the Game, Building a Team, and Growing Your Career.* New York: Harper Business, 2015.

About the Author

Ryan Eidson has worked as both an employee and in self-employed roles during his career.

Currently the Entrepreneurship Specialist at the Moberly (MO) Area Economic Development Corporation, he works with small businesses at all stages from startup to succession.

Ryan and his wife Lori have one daughter. He is also the author of *A Couple with Common Cents*.

Visit his website at **ryaneidson.com.**

**Have You Read Jack and Tabitha's
First Award-Winning Story?**

Finalist, Best Overall Design Fiction
Next Generation Indie Book Awards, 2017

2nd Place Short Story
Missouri Writers Guild President's Contest, 2017

Honorable Mention, Home Category
The Eric Hoffer Book Award, 2017

Available from all fine bookstores.
Discover more at: acouplewithcommoncents.com